Counting-Out Rhymes

Collected by
CARL WITHERS

Illustrated by
ELIZABETH RIPLEY

DOVER PUBLICATIONS, INC.
NEW YORK

Published in Canada by General Publishing Company, Ltd., 30 Lesmill Road, Don Mills, Toronto, Ontario.
Published in the United Kingdom by Constable and Company, Ltd., 10 Orange Street, London WC 2.

This Dover edition, first published in 1970, is an unabridged republication of the work originally published in 1946 by Oxford University Press, New York, under the title *Counting Out*. This edition is reprinted by special arrangement with Curtis Brown, Ltd.

Standard Book Number: 486-22414-7
Library of Congress Catalog Card Number: 77-107664

Manufactured in the United States of America
Dover Publications, Inc.
180 Varick Street
New York, N.Y. 10014

Eenie, meenie, minie, mo,
Catch a rooster by the toe.
If he hollers, let him go;
Eenie, meenie, minie, mo.

Eenie, meenie, tipsy, teeny,
Apple jack, John Sweeny;
Ootchy pootchy, Don Amootchy,
Oh, par, dar, see,
Out goes Y, O, U.

One, two, three!
Mother caught a flea.
Flea died,
Mother cried,
Out goes she.

One, two, sky blue.
All out but you.

One, two, three,
The bumblebee,
The rooster crows,
Out goes she.

One, two, three,
Tommy hurt his knee.
He couldn't slide and so he cried.
Out goes he.

One, two, three, a bumble bee
Stung a man upon his knee;
Stung a pig upon his snout.
I'll be blamed if you ain't out!

One, two, three!
Get out of my father's apple tree
Or you're IT.

One, two, three, four,
Mary at the kitchen door.
Five, six, seven, eight,
Mary at the garden gate.

One, two, three, four,
Mother scrubbed the kitchen floor.
Floor dried, mother cried,
One, two, three, four.

One, two, three, four, five,
I caught a mouse alive.
Six, seven, eight, nine, ten,
I let him go again.

One, two, three, four,
Five, six, seven.
All good children
Go to heaven.

One, two, three, four,
Five, six, seven, eight.
All bad children
Have to wait.

One, two, three, four, five,
I caught a fish; it was alive.
What made you let it go?
Because it bit my finger so.
Which finger did it bite?
The little finger on the right.

Monkey, monkey, bottle of beer.
How many monkeys have we here?
One, two, three,
You are he.

One potato, two potato,
Three potato, four;
Five potato, six potato,
Seven potato, MORE.

(The "potatoes" are the fists, which the players extend for counting. The fist which the leader points at on the word MORE is withdrawn. The leader repeats the rhyme until there is only one player left, who is It.)

One color, two color,
Three color, four;
Five color, six color,
Seven color, more.
What color is YOURS?

(When the leader says, "Yours," he
points to the child on whom the word
happens to fall, who names a color—
red, orange, yellow, etc. The leader
spells out the word, pointing as he
spells. Whoever the last letter happens
to fall on becomes It.)

One's all, two's all, zig-a-zall zan;
Bobtail nanny-goat, tittle tall tan.
Harum, scarum, merchant marum,
Sinctum, sanctum, BUCK.

Intery, mintery, cutery corn,
Apple seed and apple thorn;
Bone, briar, limber lock,
Twenty geese to make a flock.
One flew east and one flew west
And one flew over the cuckoo's nest.
One, two, three.
Out goes he.

One-ery, two-ery, ickery Ann;
Fillasy, fallasy, Nicholas John.
Quivery, quavery, Eng-ga-lish navery,
Stinkalum, stankalum, BUCK.

One-ery, two-ery, zickery, seven;
Hollow bone, cracka bone, ten or eleven.
Spin, spun, it must be done,
Twiddledum, twaddledum, twenty-one.

Inty, minty, tibblety, fig,
Deema, dima, doma, nig;
Howchy, powchy, domi, nowchy,
Hom, tom, tout.
Olligo, bolligo, boo;
Out goes YOU.

Itsa, bitsa, tootsa, la
Falla-melinka, linka, la
Falla-malu, falla-mila
Falla-melinka, linka, la.

Ibbity, bibbity, sibbity, Sam,
Ibbity, bibbity, canal boat;
Up the river, down the river,
Out goes Y, O, U.

Ibbity, bibbity, sibbity, say;
Ibbity, bibbity, vanilla.
Dictionary
Down the ferry,
Fun, fun,
American gum,
Eighteen hundred
Ninety-one.

Ibbity, bibbity, shindo;
My mother was washing the window.
The window got broke
My mother got soak,
Ibbity bibbity shindo.
    My mother told me
    To take this one.

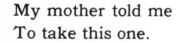

Ish, fish, codfish.
How many fish are in your golden dish?

Ikkamy, dukkamy, alligar mole,
Dick slew alligar slum;
Hukka pukka, Peter's gum—
Francis!

Ecka, decka, donie, crecka,
Ecka, decka, do;
Ease, cheese, butter, bread,
Out goes you!

Butter, levi, boni, stry,
Hair, brit, brof, nack;
We, wo, wack.
O, U, T spells
Out goes he.

Eggs, butter, cheese, bread,
Stick, stock, stone, dead.
Set him up, set him down,
Set him in the old man's crown.

Hickory, dickory, dare,
The pig flew up in the air.
A man in brown
Brought him down,
Hickory, dickory, dare.

Oka, bocca, stona crocka,
Oka, bocca, boo:
In comes Uncle Sam,
And out goes you.

Hoky, poky, winky, wum,
How do you like your taters done?
Snip, snap, snorum,
High populorum.
Kate go scratch it,
You are OUT.

Cricky, cracky, craney, crow,
I went to the well to wash my toe.
High and low, out you go,
Cricky, cracky, craney, crow.

INDIAN COUNTING

Een, teen, tether, fether, fip,
Sather, lather, gother, dather, dix;
Een-dix, teen-dix, tether-dix,
    fether-dix, bumpit;
Een-bumpit, teen-bumpit, tether-bumpit,
    fether-bumpit, gig-it.

> This is often called "Indian counting"
> but it's really based on Welsh numer-
> als.

Allalong, allalong, linkey, loo,
Merry goes, one, merry goes, two,
Allalong, allalong, linkey, loo,
Merry goes, one, merry goes, two,
Allalong, allalong, linkey, loo,
Merry goes, one, merry goes, two,
I'll lay, a wager, with any, of you,
That's all, my marks,
    make thirty, and two.

A poor little boy without any shoe:
One, two, three, and out goes you.

Andy, Mandy,
Sugar candy,
Out goes he.

Pig's snout,
Walk out.

Three men driving cattle,
Can't you hear their money rattle?
One, two, three,
Out goes he.

Sinner, sinner,
Come to dinner,
Half past two.
Fried potatoes,
Alligators,
Out goes you.

Tommy Tinker sat on a klinker;
Then he began to cry,
"Ma, Ma!"
That poor little innocent guy.

As I went up the apple tree
All the apples fell on me.
I took one, my brother took another,
And we both jumped over the bridge
    together.
One, two, three,
Out goes she.

All the monkeys in the zoo
Had their tails painted blue.
One, two, three—Out goes you.

Once an apple met an apple;
Said the apple to the apple,
"Why the apple don't the apple
Get the apple *out* of here?"

We had a piece of pie
Made out of rye,
And 'possum was the meat.
The crust was tough,
But we had enough
And more than all could eat.
E, A, T, *eat*.

Monkey, monkey, sitting on a fence,
Trying to make a dollar out of fifteen
cents.
One, two, three,
Out goes he.

My mother and your mother
    lived across the way—
Two-fourteen East Broadway.
Every night they'd have a fight
And this is what they'd say:
    Acka backa soda cracka,
    Acka backa boo.
    If your father wants tobacka,
    Out goes Y, O, U.

I know something I won't tell:
Three little rabbits in a peanut shell.
One can sing and one can dance,
One can make a pair of pants.
O, U, T spells out goes she.

RIDDLE

Four diddle-diddle-danders,
Two stiff-stiff-standers,
Two lookers, and a switch-about.
An old cow and you're It!

Fireman, fireman,
Number eight,
Hit his head against the gate.
The gate flew in, the gate flew out;
That's the way he put the fire out.
O, U, T spells OUT—
And out you go.

Yellow cornmeal,
Red tomato,
Ribbon cane;
Sweet potato;
Round melon,
Ripe persimmon,
Little goober-peas.

Engine, engine, number nine,
Running on the railroad line.
If it's polished, it will shine,
Engine, engine, number nine.

Polly wants a cracker,
Polly wants a ball,
Polly wants you to be
First of all.

Polly wants a cracker,
Polly wants a ball.
Polly wants you to be
Second of all (etc.).

John says to John,
"How much are your geese?"
John says to John,
"Twenty cents apiece."
John says to John,
"That's too dear."
John says to John,
"Get out of here!"

My father built a little red schoolhouse.
How many nails did he put in it?

(The word *it* determines who is It, or
the child on whom the word falls may
say a number—which is then used in
counting around the circle.)

Three potatoes in a pot,
Take one out and leave it hot.

Tit, tat, toe,
Round I go;
If I don't miss
I'll stop on this.

A, B, C, D,
Tell your age to me.

(The child pointed to on the word
me gives his age. Then the leader
counts, pointing in turn to the children. When he gets to the number re-
presenting the age given, the child at
whom he points becomes It.)

All around the butter dish,
One, two, three;
If you want a pretty girl,
Just pick me.
Blow the bugles,
Beat the drums,
Tell me when your birthday comes.

(The child on whom the word *comes*
falls gives his birthdate: the day of the
month. Without moving, the players
stand until the leader has counted
around the circle till the given number
is reached. The child on whom it falls
is It.)

Apple, peach, pear, plum,
When does your birthday come?

The sky is blue.
How old are you?

(The player on whom *you* falls gives
his age. This number is then used for
counting out.)

Ish tish, tash tish,
What color do you wish?

(The child pointed to on *wish* names
a color, which is then spelled out by
the leader, who points to the children
in turn as he spells. The last letter
determines It.)

As I went up the apple tree,
All the apples fell on me.
Bake a pudding, bake a pie,
Did you ever tell a lie?
Yes you did, you know you did,
You broke your mother's teapot lid.
L, I, D,—that spells lid.

My mother and your mother,
    hanging out the clothes;
My mother hit your mother
    in the nose.
What color blood came out?

(O, R, A, N, G, E; or any other color.)

Red, white and blue—
All out but you.

Ink, a-bink, a bottle of ink.
The cork fell out and—you're It!

My father has a horse to shoe.
How many nails do you think will do?

(Each child hastens to choose a number smaller than the number of players. When only this number is left, the child who must choose it becomes It.)

Rich, Rich, fell in the ditch,
And never got back till half-past six.
My mother told me you are It.

Frank, Frank, turned the crank;
His mother came out
    and gave him a spank.

Wash the lady's dishes,
Hang them on the bushes;
When the bushes start to crack
Hang them on a donkey's back.
When the donkey starts to run
Shoot him with a leather gun.

Miller, miller, dusty pole,
How many sacks have you stole?
Twenty-five and a peck.
Hang up the miller by his neck.

Jean, Jean,
Dressed in green,
Went downtown
To eat icecream.
How many dishes did she eat?
One, two, three, four, five.

Little dog sat on the porch,
And Bingo was his name:
      B, I, N, G, O,
      B, I, N, G, O,
      B, I, N, G, O,
Bingo was his name.

Jack, Jack, sat on a tack,
And went to bed with a sore back.
O, U, T, and out goes he.

Tobacco, hic,
'Twill make you sick;
Tobacco, sick,
'Twill make you hic.

A knife and a fork,
A bottle and a cork,
That's the way
To spell New York.

Sam, Sam, the soft soap man,
Washed his face in a frying pan,
Combed his hair with a wagon-wheel,
And died with a toothache in his heel.

Peter Matrimity was a fine water-man;
He steals hens and puts them in pens.
Some lay eggs and some lay none:
Whitefoot, Specklefoot,
Trip, trap,
And begone——
Old hen.

My old man and I fell out,
And what do you think it was about?
He had money and I had none
And that's the way the quarrel begun.
Go O, U, T—out!

Policeman, policeman, don't catch me!
Catch that boy behind the tree.
He stole apples, I stole none;
Put him in the jail-house, just for fun.

Billy, Billy Burst——
Who speaks first?

(The one who speaks first, after this is
shouted is out; the rhyme is repeated
until only one is left, and he is It.)

Last night and the night before
Twenty-four robbers were at my door.
Wake up, wake up, ginger blue,
And don't be afraid of the bugaboo!

As I went by the garden gate,
I met a little rattle snake;
He ate so much of jelly cake,
It made his little belly ache.

Fishes, fishes, in the brook,
Papa catch them with a hook,
Mama fry them in a pan,
Johnny eat them like a man.

With a C and a sigh
And a Constanti
With a nople and a pople
And a Constantinople

Yesterday upon the stair
I saw a man who wasn't there.
He wasn't there again today——
Oh how I wish he'd stay away.

The first lieutenant he was so neat,
He stopped the battle to wash his feet.

W, double-O, D, WOOD;
    Sockety peck!
Run round the limb
And stick your bill in—
    WOODPECKER!

F for finis
I for inis
N for nocklebone
I for Isaac
S for Silas—Silverspoon

FINGERS ON THE TABLE

All the children place both index fingers on the table, and the following rhyme is recited by the leader, who points to a finger on each accented word. The finger on which the last word falls is withdrawn, and the rhyme is repeated until there is only one finger (or one player's fingers) left on the table—that player is It.

Intery, mintery, cutery, corn,
Apple seed and apple thorn;
Wire briar, limber lock,
Twelve geese in a flock,
Sit and sing by a spring,
O, U, T, spells out and in again.
Over yonder steep hills
Where my father he dwells,
He has jewels, he has rings
And very many pretty things.
Strike Jack, Lick Tom
Blow the bellow——
Black finger out of the GAME.

You're IT,
You've got a fit,
And don't know how
To get out of it.